Crooked Doesn't Mean Broken

Waldrena Thomas- Robinson

DEDICATION

This book is dedicated to women all over the world.

We live in a world where time is relative; either moving too fast or too slow. Which caused many of us to never stay still long enough to build stable relationships.

How has it become so easy to forget that as relational beings we are to learn to interact, engage, share our thoughts, and love those around us.

I have watched from the sidelines long enough and witnessed first-hand how multiple friendships have crumbled.

Yet no-one feels the need to take the initiative and repair them.

As a result, they remain torn allowing hostility to settle in and question why many of us are broken.

Take a journey with me as we find out the root cause of why this cancerous agent called bitterness continues to feast on us ultimately destroying the bond, we once had as sisters.

Withhold not good from them to whom it is due, when it is in the power of thine hand to do it. -Proverbs 3:37

TABLE OF CONTENTS

ACKNOWLEDGMENTS

Precious Savior,

Oh, how I marvel at the beauty of who you are.

To honor you have been the greatest achievement of all time.

So once again we're on this journey that seems to never end.

I count it a blessing that you have chosen an unworthy vessel as

myself to carry this flaming instrument known as my pen.

My goal has been to leave this world empty; taking nothing to

the grave.

For this treasure you have placed inside of me is far too precious

to be buried beneath the earth and turned into ash when so many

others can be saved.

Which is why I have dedicated my life to being an open and

willing receptacle for you to use for your glory.

As you speak, I will listen, prompting the anointing to take over

causing me to write the words you have boldly given me to share.

There is nothing else I rather do then bask in your presence as you

allow your spirit to immerse these pages with words that have no

choice but to come to life.

I will never take for granted this amazing gift.

Without you none of this would be possible; so, Father may

the words you have given me to write penetrate the hearts of all

that would read them..

Sincerely your servant,

Waldrena

My beautiful daughters: Amaya, Micaila & Malia

The greatest gifts in this life would be the three of you.

You have continued to push me to always be greater than

the day before.

My prayer for the three of you would be to go after your dreams,

despite the obstacles that may come your way.

My beautiful babies there is so much to discover beyond the sky.

I love you all

Mommy

My husband: Michael G. Robinson

This fifteen-year ride has been utterly amazing, and I cannot

imagine enjoying this journey without you.

In your eyes I have seen the endless possibilities of what we are

to attain.

Your love's unconditional, your dedication to our family

is priceless for you have demonstrated it effortlessly.

My dearest I will forever be grateful for the role you occupy my

life. Love your wife, Waldrena

My parents: James Thomas & Mary Thomas-Engram

I admire you both for your strength to push through despite the many hurdles in your path.

You are truly an example of what it means to never give up.

Two imperfect beings taking parenting seriously by instilling in your children the importance of making a difference.

I love you both today and always,

Your daughter, Waltsdream

My siblings: JT, Timothy, Demetrius, Quenton, James & Thelma

We all have been through the toughest of storms and yet came out unscathed is truly a blessing within itself.

Only the Lord knew what was in store for his children.

Each of you have touched my life in ways you may never know.

Your sister: Waldrena

Special thanks to: Sarah Penney (unsplash.com) for the beautiful book cover. For my mentors, family, & friends 'words cannot express how much you all mean to me. I appreciate you for you being there every step of the way. -I love you

Preface

The word relationship is a board scope of how two or more people can relate and function, it is not placed inside a box to be categorized into one area.

Meanwhile friendships hone specifically on an intimate trust between two people.

When deciding what my next writing assignment would be I immediately thought of the torn relationship between women.

We did not seem to understand the SHIPS we had with one another, so we struggled with the value they carried.

Which explains why we are so quick to tear each other down oppose to building each other up.

How being jealous and bitter have caused us to hate one another without a cause?

I am sure most women rather in our past or our present can admit they have bottled up emotions and without any warning that bottle begins to shatter causing toxic waste to spill over and contaminant anything or anyone in its path.

Resulting in negativity as it starts to trinkle down into relationships and immediately poison us to the core.

It is easier to focus on the downfall of others then it is to build one another up.

However, I beg to differ I have always been told the only time you should look down on a man/woman is when you're picking them up.

My sister's crown was written to give us a better understanding that crooked does not mean broken, but merely that we all have had some bouts with life which took us through some things, so now we're taking the strength we have left to hold on.

If your sister's crown (life, situation, or appearance) seems to have slightly tilted to the left do not be so quick to share it with others but do what you can to assist without expecting anything in return.

It's only then you'll be able to enjoy the beauty of not only being blessing to others, but also yourself.

CHAPTER ONE: CLIPPED WING

High in the sky with so much promise yet we find it hard to soar.

What has cause us to lose confidence in our ability to gage the

magnitude of purpose to succeed in this life.

Was it the unbelief that started to overwhelm you, or the

naysayers that pointed out that your wing had been clipped.

My friend, please don't allow small disabilities to stop you from

pursuing your goals and living out your dreams.

Clipped does not mean you cannot fly it just means you need to

be trimmed.

Trimmed so that the new and improved you could grow.

There was no way you could remain as you were because it

would limit your ability to become the phenomenal being you

were destined to be.

It is nothing you could do in your own strength, but someone far

greater.

The Creator had made it his business to trim individuals from your life simply because he knew you could not do it on your own.

He knew fear would cause you to believe you'd hurt someone's feelings and before he would allow them to prevent you from reaching the next level, he did what was best.

If I have said it once…I have said it a thousand times "Everyone that started with you will not finish with you," and you must be okay with that.

As your sister and friend, I am here to assist you, not belittle or cause you to stumble.

So many of us do not understand our role and that of those around us, and as a result, we have replaced being compassionate with being heartless.

The things our peers spoke to us in confidence we have aired out publicly without ever batting an eye.

The world was such a different place, time, and safe space full of endless possibilities now it thrives on being judgmental of others, feuds of all kinds, senseless drama, deaths and division to say the least.

The toxicity of this environment has caused the crowns we once wore proudly to not only become tarnish but lose its value.

Being judgmental should break your heart that hatred has found its way inside of you.

The need to upstage those around you seems to continue being the driving force that leads to dead-end streets…..streets that are dark, lonely, and desolate.

The farther you travel along the more you're lead to lean unto your own understanding seeking navigation directions from everything/ everyone, only to be reroute back to where you started.

So, if the Creator has already planned a way of escape why are we still waiting for him reach back and personally grab us by the hand and lead us out?

What happened to the zeal that made us confident in who we were; not to mention the determination to see that no sister would be left behind?

We knew what made us resilient, but somewhere in the shuffle we have lost it.

Despite what anyone says there has always been enough pie for us all to enjoy.

There was never any need to fight amongst each in order to get a slice.

I ask that you dig deep within not only in these pages, but within yourself to truly see the purpose that was planted inside of you.

Our daughters are counting on us to leave some gems behind so they don't find themselves repeating the same cycle.

CHAPTER TWO: WOMAN IN THE MIRROR

Tap, Tap, Tap it is me your reflection (known as the woman in the mirror) it is imperative that you answer before this mirror shatters into pieces leaving you to expose things you desperately wanted concealed.

Forgive me but I have noticed you along with many others have stop embracing who you are, and how you see yourselves?

You have allowed others to make you believe you are of a less pedigree than your counterparts.

Yes, your outward appearance shows the dimples in your curves, your natural beauty shows a few blemishes, your teeth are not as straight as some, your hair is kinky at times, while your wardrobe can use a little upgrading amongst many other things.

However, those things should never cause you to feel less beautiful.

Show the world that you are more than the natural eye can see, you have a voice that brings an awareness of what needs to be changed, how it will take all of us to help those that have been pushed to the wayside, that we are better together than apart.

You have spent countless hours waiting for this moment to shine and showcase all your hard work and now this is the moment we've been waiting for.

What are you going to do?

Before the curtain could open you did the unthinkable...

You ran away and hid.

My sister, when will you muster up enough courage to step up to the center stage and realize you have something to bring to the table?

It's not what you wear that will speak to the crowd of people, but when you open your mouth and speak from your soul that will penetrate their hearts and it's in that very moment they will realize more about themselves then they ever imagined.

So many times, they wrestled with trying to find their true identity wanted to say those same words to themselves of how they mattered and you allowed fear to cause you to run away.

You have a lot of work to do my sister more now than ever.

There are hundreds maybe even thousands waiting for you to step out and take your rightful place.

Make your voice heard others are counting on you.

Now to the rest of them: the next time you see yourself or even another woman for that matter and it does not appear they have that barbie doll look, department store fragrance, or share your same thoughts do not be in such a hurry to judge.

We all have a story and it's up to us if we choose to share what was written.

It saddens me that many of us look at the cover and draw our own conclusion.

Instead of collecting all the facts to shed some insight on what was going on we waste no time putting on our gear to immediately assassinate the character of the person who has not only written the story, but has suffered through the pages.

No-one wakes up one day and choose to be in a broken state of mind there is a much bigger underlining issue than what is seen.

Our species can be so superficial at times, always seeming to find the worst about others to make themselves feel accomplished or highly esteemed.

Pulling back the covers of someone's past even for a moment hoping to discover hidden hurt is despicable.

Have you ever thought there must be a reason they buried it in the first place?

I believe as women there's tons of layers attached to us that would take years to fully uncover.

Years simply because we will always find a way to hold back just enough so that we do not unearth everything due to the fear that others would look at us in a different light if those things are finally released.

I am sure you have heard the saying:

"My business anit everybody business."

Well, I believe that if it is going to help save a life then it is our business.

Which brings me to this if you or someone you know have been experiencing hurt, have lost their zeal for the things they once loved, or even have started to isolate themselves from those close to them it's our job to step in.

Not stepping in to have something to gossip about later, but to be there as a listening ear or a shoulder to cry on.

I hope by sharing this with you it would cause you to start making some well needed adjustments.

Until next time stay true to yourself and those around you.

CHAPTER THREE:

REFRESH, RESTORE & RENEW

In this chapter I'm going to need your assistance to help me understand the dynamics of a few things.

Even though we're of the same species we have a problem with being okay with others placing us in a variety of classes, instead of finding ways to restore, refresh and renew one another?

We never stopped to think how much more detrimental it was than to speak life into those that needed it the most.

I hate to keep you waiting so without any further delay grab your spoons because we're about to dig in.

There are several classes of women although I have not listed them all, I have given a brief description solely to use for educational purposes.

Class A: these types of women are solely concerned about their following on different social media outlets, being materialistic, updating the latest posts, but will never admit they struggle with low self-esteem.

Class B: feels entitled, has a bad attitude, close minded, allows others to think for them ultimately causing them to miss out on opportunities and or relationships.

Class C: needs to be validated because they struggle with being enough to themselves and those around them due to past hurt from former relationships/ friendships.

Class: D: are those that's often overlooked because they don't appear to have beauty or intelligence.

Class: E: these women are confident in who they are, their leaders prepared to take the world by storm.

I hope by you reading those descriptions it caused you to see things more precisely.

Rather you agree or not there's a lot of work we have to do in order to put an end to the hate and bitterness that many women around the world have felt at one time or another.

How often have we saw friendships/ relationships deteriorate due to betrayal?

Betrayal is breaking or violating of a person's trust or confidence, of a moral standard.

Why has it been okay to take the very thing someone entrusted us with and broadcast it publicly?

I'll respond it's not and never would be.

As women we already have a hard enough time as it is trying to jungle ourselves, life, responsibilities, and so many other things. As sisters when one of us is hurting, down, lost, and confused our job is to restore her better or greater than she was before.

Just because life has beat some of us down to the point not only are our crowns crooked, but a part of it is missing.

We don't need anyone getting close to us to use as leverage over our heads, or to make them feel better about their situation.

Ladies it's too many of us out here in the world to just carry on with our lives and see our sister's hurting and do nothing about it. It doesn't take much to help restore those in need.

We're better together so let's start replacing our conceitedness with confidence, our vanity with value, worthless to worthwhile, bashing to beautifying in doing so we'll recognize not only does it strengthens our unit as women, but helps restore the missing part of our sister and her crown.

CHAPTER FOUR: MISSING JEWEL
(UNDERSTANDING YOU)

One of the biggest challenges one has ever had to face would be understanding who they are and what they bring to the table. The reason is simply because they have accepted what family, friends, or even outsiders have expressed who they were and never felt the need to correct them.

For starters our parents made sure we understood their expectations from the gate and everything else followed suit. When leaving home, we had to conduct ourselves in a certain manner because we reflected them, around our family they saw us as entertaining and fun, friends we were exciting and adventurous, co-workers and associates we were laid back, to our children annoying, our spouses their helpmeets, while to outsiders we were never enough no matter what we'd do or say. Rather some of us agree with this or not the problem that seem to constantly arise is how we continue to forget who we are by being so caught up in how others perceived us.

It has never been about what they called you…it's what you've always answered to.

How many of us have allowed others to call us the wrong name, speak senseless babble over our lives, tell us how insufficient we are, and yet we still refuse to correct them.

Just because it was spoken over you "that you'll never amount to anything" did not mean you had/ must accept it.

All this ever did was cause negativity to set in making you question everything.

What is the purpose of my existence?

What makes me different?

What will be my greatest accomplishment?

Often, we tend to lose ourselves over time because we never notice the chipping that occurs.

Chippings are described as giving so much of yourself to the point you have nothing left, loving someone more than you love yourself, believing that others know what's best for you, or just refusing to acknowledge your worth and what you could contribute.

When did we start to lose ourselves in the shuffle of life?

To understand who we are; we must understand whose we are.

The bible says in Psalms 139: 13-14: For thou hast possessed my reins: thou hast covered me in my mother's womb.

I will praise thee; for I am fearfully and wonderfully made: marvellous are thy works; and that my soul knoweth right well.

I once read that we were created with great reverenced, heart-felt interest, and respected to be unique and set apart.

We have been handmade and it's something about how we were made that made us fearful by those that did not understand what we truly possessed inside.

You are the most important being in all the earth and have been separated from the day you were born.

Which is why you must dig deep and discover what makes you laugh, bring you joy, peace, and what drives you to be great.

It's okay that you're different it's what makes you stand out from everyone else around you.

In the words of my late pastor:

"Be you everyone else is already taken"

CHAPTER FIVE:

EMBRACING YOUR PAST

Depends on who you ask embracing your past could either cause you to think of a special moment spent with the person (s) you loved or recall a traumatic experience you desperately wanted to forget, either way it'll allow you to look at life through a different lens and hope whatever the outcome you will be able to live with it.

As your friend and cheerleader, I want to encourage you although there are some things you wish you could erase or request a do-over I need you to understand that those things needed to occur in order to mold you into the person you are today.

Life has always been about the experience.

Although you will never forget what you went through, its important to accept it and move on.

Embrace it for you have made it through that once troubled place of sadness and have found happiness at the end of the tunnel.

It was not to prove the naysayers wrong, but to prove to yourself that you are indeed an overcomer.

What did not kill you only made you stronger.

Stronger because you learned to use the pain that was sent to destroy you as ammo, instead of allowing the pain to use you causing you to kill the potential of greatness that was embedded into you the day you were born.

Although your past maybe traumatic and even frightening at times: believe in yourself enough to know you're guaranteed to reach the finish line if you don't give up.

Not everything you endured was to keep you defeated and miserable.

Everyone has one (a past that is) rather they were deemed good, bad, or even ugly.

Whatever you chose to do with it would be solely up to you.

Just think of your past as your twin. It's looks like you, sounds like you, and even walks like you the only difference: one is who you once were the other is the new and improved you.

You are much wiser and mature than you were as an adolescent.

Could it be true your past only seem to appear when it wanted something from you by keeping you in a stagnant place and stopping your growth?

It's time you start tapping into your full potential if you plan to succeed.

Am I saying its bad to for one to recall a memory, of course not. Remembering is embedded into the core of your mind it causes you to recall where you once were and realize only by the grace of God you made it out.

There are many examples of why it's important that we move forward and the one that sticks out the most Genesis chapter 19:17, 24-26 the bible states: 17) And it came to pass, when they had brought them forth abroad, that he said, **escape for thy life; look not behind thee, neither stay thou in the plain; escape to the mountain, lest thou be consumed.**

24) Then the Lord rained upon Sodom and upon Gomorrah brimstone and fire from the Lord out of heaven;

25) And he overthrew those cities, and all the plain, and all the inhabitants of the cities, and that which grew upon the ground.

26) **But his wife looked back from behind him, and she became a pillar of salt.**"

It wasn't enough for us to leave our old neighborhoods, those we grew up around but follow the instructions we were given once we left those places and people.

The Lord and his angels knew that Lot and his family weren't going to forget the people, where they came from, and what drove them to have to pick up and leave suddenly.

All he wanted was to be obeyed and trusted for he knew that if he didn't step in when he did so many would have been corrupted. Looking back was going to warp their way of thinking physically and mentally.

The sad part in all of this there's always going to be one to test the waters: one that doesn't think a simple glance is going to cost them to lose everything including their life, but it does.

Many of us have allowed our past to impact our future because we couldn't press forward.

It's easier to look back to a familiar place even for a moment then it is to move forward in the uncertainty of what is waiting for us on the other side.

Our past has closed doors for a reason and going back for even a brief second could cause us to become trapped and ultimately lose the key to our future forever.

In the words of the late Duranice Pace:

"When helping you is hurting me, keeping you is killing me, blessing you is cursing me when my PAST won't allow me to PASS.

My question is what are you going to do?

You must decide is it worth allowing your past to overshadow your future? A future that is full of discovery, adventure, and brighter as the day goes on or will you continue to walk in circles as the children in the wilderness and wonder what could have been.

Think about this for a moment, have you ever wondered where the richest place in the world was located.

If your answer was yes I can't wait to share.

Can you believe it's the cemetery.

How many people do you know or have heard about that have had the potential to be great doctors, lawyers, chemists, engineers, but died before ever achieving the dream.

I don't want to be cruel when I say this, but a lot of this stemmed from them continuing to remain in their comfort zone and doing the bear minimal because its familiar oppose to stepping out in the deep and taking a chance.

The failure of anything is if you never try, not stepping out and not succeeding the first time around.

CHAPTER SIX:

BUILDING YOUR FAITH

Just as the saying goes Rome wasn't built in a day, neither is building your faith both requires time and patience.

The Creator have paved a path for today, put an end to yesterday, and will walk ahead of us to prepare for tomorrow. He knows firsthand what is needed to not only build our foundation, but our belief.

Tearing down seems to be easy, while building seems to take a lifetime just know it takes effort, consistency, and being placed into tough situations that would test everything we know or thought we knew in order for us to build a stable foundation. Once that foundation is built there we will experience growth of expansion that would not only enlarge our territory, but will give us the knowledge to overcome whatever comes our way. The bible states in Hebrews 11: 1 Now faith is the substance of things hoped for, the evidence of things not seen.

However, it doesn't stop there in the book of Proverbs 3:5-6 the word also instructs us to Trust in the Lord with all thine heart and lean not unto thine own understanding.

In all thy ways acknowledge him, and he shall direct thy paths.

It's easy to trust the Creator when the things we're asking for are minute, but what happens when it's not and our waiting isn't only tested but also tried in the fire.

Will we have enough faith to stand when those requests start to manifest?

Although we know the Creator hasn't created us to fear, it doesn't stop us from doing it.

The only weapon we have to combat worrying is to have faith in knowing that the creator is at work on our behalf.

My sister building your faith isn't going to be easy, but trust the process that it will be worth establishing.

We all face storms in our lives and some more vicious than others, but trust and believe we all go through at some time or another and it's in those times we grab a hold of our faith.

As we doubt it becomes a weapon the enemy uses against us to shake our foundation and attack us since we've willingly disarmed ourselves due to our lack of confidence.

The bible says in James 1:6 But let him ask in faith, nothing wavering. For he that wavereth is like a wave of the sea driven with the wind and toss.

My sister I don't want this to be your story, so I have listed a few pointers in hopes of getting, you get started…

- Set aside some alone time with you and the Creator

- Constantly engage yourself in hearing God's word

- Examine the scriptures and allow the Lord to speak to you

- Pray regularly (it doesn't have to be long and drawn out) for the Creator knows what you have need of.

- Have hope in the process

Doubting is never an option despite how things appear.

The Creator has always been faithful, trustworthy, and a promise keeper, that is who He is and will always be.

We must embrace this truth if we plan to develop strong faith.

Never let the enemy see you sweat….

You have already been given the victory you just gotta stay the course and refuse to give in.

Trust the enemy knows when you're weak and will use it to his advantage.

Do you remember there were several occurrences in which he (Satan, the enemy. or whatever you call him) tried to tempt our Lord?

If you're not familiar with any of them, I'll list some for you.

After he had fasted for forty days and forty nights and was hungry how the deceiver came and said "If you are the Son of God, tell these stones to become bread. (Matthew 4:2-3) Another time he took him to the holy city and had him stand on the highest point of the temple and said "Throw yourself down. For it is written:
He will command his angels concerning you, and they will lift you up in their hands, so that you will not strike your foot against a stone. (Matthew 4:5) When those things didn't work, he (the enemy) started to kick it up a notch by taking our Lord to a very high mountain and showed him all the kingdoms of the world and their splendor.

Being his crafty self, he says:

All this I give you if you will bow down and worship me.

This idiot seems to have forgotten that our father is a King.

There is nothing he (the deceiver) can give us that we can't attain from our Father in Heaven.

For the bible says in Psalms 84 that no good thing will he withhold from them that walk uprightly.

I mentioned all of that to say it's important to not allow ourselves to lose our footing: even when things begin to become too much use your heel to break up the soil beneath you and remain sown. The Lord sees us and will never allow us to be plucked out of his hand nor from the root and die prematurely for he will allow us to bloom in the very place we were planted to show others the beauty of his power.

Power that with just one word will change the course of our situation.

Who wouldn't want to trust someone with that much control?

CHAPTER SEVEN:

JEWELRY STORE

My dear sister you must understand the importance of who you are in order to reach the place the Creator desires you to be.

I can only imagine the course you have travelled in your life good, bad, or indifferent.

You mustn't count yourself out of the game there is still time for you to make a final play.

A few months ago, I was given a revelation about myself in a way that blew my mind.

It may sound a little over the top but give me a minute to explain.

Sometimes we wonder what type of people we encounter in this life, those that are seasonal (temporary) or those that would stick around for a lifetime (Lifers).

Lifers are those that will weather the storm with you no matter what comes your way. They have taken their vows seriously not just made it a cliché by saying they'll always be there unlike those that do and when you need them the most they're nowhere to be found.

Although scattered there are many lifers still around today.

To understand our worth, we must ask ourselves some deep questions rather we want to be real about the responses we give or not.

All I ask is that you bear with me so that I can simplify just what I meant in order to give you a deeper and clearer understanding of this topic.

When you enter a jewelry store there are tons of jewelry displayed behind a glass counter, although there are many costly items displayed ask yourself this:

Where are the most valuable pieces stored?

The answer is a safe or vault, but why?

Simply because many can't afford it, while others could cause damage due to their lack of experience in handling precious jewels, or even worst it could be placed in the hands of those that don't have the mindset to give you the care you deserve.

Which caused me to analyze this theory and put into perspective what was happening inside my head and find a way to express it on paper for others to understand as well.

Think of your life as a jewelry store; there are many people that are going to enter into it (your life that is).

Those that are spectators, rejectors, and passovers.

The spectators are the ones that the clerk ask "Hello, can I help you? They respond by saying "No thank you I'm just browsing." These types of people are only there to find out what's going on in your life, they aren't there to stick around long term.

Then in walks the rejector: the one that has it going on, that have the means but refuse to invest into you for whatever reason.

Lastly, they're the passovers: these are those that no-one pays attention to, looks down on because it appears they're going to waste your time.

Don't be so quick to judge a book by its cover.

Those passovers the ones you overlooked because of their appearance were indeed your person.

Not only could they afford to make a purchase (willing to invest into you), knew how to take care of you, the value you possessed but would always cherish the very essence of who you were.

My sister I said that to say this:

Not everyone is there to be an asset to your life some are there only to see what you have going on and use you, others have the means but refuse to pour into what you need, whatever, the case it has always been the one we passed up that had our best interest at heart, knew our worth and how to handle us the most. Stop attaching yourself to those that do not mean you any good. The Creator has molded you to be the rarest type of gem in the world and made it so that not everyone could have access to you. Not that you are perfect, but that you have something valuable. You have been set apart placed into a vault until just the right time. Understand your worth is priceless and its imperative not to allow anything or anyone tamper with your refinement process.

It has taken a lot of effort to get you to where you are today which is why you must stay the course so that no-one would be able to stop the potential that would come from it.

Face it not everyone is going to shine the same as you, and its okay. What the Lord has for me is for me, what he has for you is for you and that's how it is.

CHAPTER EIGHT:

MY SISTER'S CROWN

I am not here to beat you over the head, gossip about your shortcomings, or dig into your past about the person you once were.

As your sister know you can trust me to be there when you feel like giving up, throwing in the towel, or even the times you feel you've lost your way.

However, I will never be the person to sweep your dirt under the rug, and not hold you accountable.

Part of fixing your crown will be:

- To cover you, not expose you

- Help not hinder you

- Bless not curse you

- Build you up not tear you down

- Walk with you, not on top of you

- Add to not take away from you

Not everyone will be honest with you out of fear they would offend you so they will ultimately tell you what you want to hear in order to spare your feelings.

I, on the other hand, feel it's my duty to tell you the truth because I not only care about you, but I also want to do whatever I can to push you to be greater and if that comes off as being offensive sorry but not sorry.

To kick it up a notch I have also provided you with a few definitions to drive this theory home.

Covering: means to protect them from being attacked.

Helping: is providing someone with what is useful or necessary to achieve an end.

Bless: To ask God to look favorably on.

Build up: To make a person or their body stronger.

Walk with: to accompany or escort.

Add to: Make greater.

Anything outside of these aren't displaying the true attributes of a sister.

We should always embrace the strength we have as women. How awesome it is to be able to communicate with just a simple glance or slight gesture.

We are powerful creatures with many gifts rather that's multitasking, helping others when they fall short, or simply stepping out and creating change which has no other choice but to make an impact in this world.

The issue I often have would be how some of us seem to only assist if they can be returned the favor down the line.

Causing you to wonder if their intentions were truly given from a genuine heart or to simply announce the deed (rather good or bad) to all that cared to listen about their superwoman rescue in order to receive some sort of praise.

If you notice your sister rather by blood, adoption, or someone you met in passing crown has to shifted slightly to the right, barely hanging on, and you were there to support that's good, but please don't be the type to constantly remind that individual every time you saw them it was due to your help that they were able to make it through those hard times.

No-one should have to remind you that being a woman is tough enough, and there are going to be times when our crowns are going to become a little difficult to keep on and may need adjusting from time to time.

However, can you do us all the favor and just help a sister out instead of just babbling out to everyone that the crown was twisted or slightly tampered with. I'm sure you'd expect the same.

We all are striving for the same thing and that's to leave our mark in this world, without having to worry about our past, it's been buried for a reason and for someone to dig it up to use as leverage in order to make themselves seem more prestigious is quite baffling to me.

Chapter Nine

The gathering place

In this mini guide we have sipped on a chilled beverage, sampled an appetizer, ate our entrée' now it's time to gather around for the good stuff a small bite of dessert.

As you know the dessert is the sweetest part, which is why we had to digest all what we had eaten before in order to make room for what was coming.

With that my hope is that this guide has opened many of you to understand the importance of restoring lost and broken relationships amongst women around the world.

How the lack of connections have impacted our circles and communities.

We can't even socialize without negativity being the center of our conversation.

I don't know about you, but I feel that spewing deadly venom has caused the potential of growth to not only become stagnant but also die.

Why has it been so easy to criticize each other when there are some of us that know firsthand how it feels to be ostracized for no apparent reason.

How dare we look down on someone else not to mention our sister that seems to have been dragged through the mill, and only wanted someone to show compassion and concern for what they have gone through.

Call it society, friendships or relationships that went sour whatever the case we have no excuse to demean, assassinate someone's character, or make them feel unworthy.

The ultimate lesson I want you to take away from this book isn't to point fingers, but to bring an awareness of what seems to be the driving force behind the bitterness that has caused a hedge between our sisters.

Although, our opinions, thoughts, and the way we handle business may differ from time to time at the end of the day we must find a way to bring our differences to the table, put the hurt behind us and help restore the brokenness we've all witnessed at some point or another in our lives.

Every day is another day to start afresh, it will never be enough to just have one encounter, walk away scot-free, nor is it something to be crossed off your bucket list and move on.

Fixing your sister's crown is a way of living.

You never know when you or someone else's crown (situation) would need to be adjusted.

Each one of us have come from various walks of life which is why we must approach every situation differently.

All have or will experience circumstances in this life that can't be handled on our own, in that instant you must reach out and grab a hold of the nearest branch (your sister), tie a knot and hold on.

This branch will provide stability and assurance to cross over to the other side without any mishaps.

No matter what anyone says branches are very vital.

You never know if it would be utilized in order to help build, or even become a crutch to help support you.

Now please understand I would never suggest that you do all the leg work by helping someone and they never lift a finger to help themselves.

However, I am saying if you see someone that needs a hand up, not hand out you should assist.

Pride has caused many to believe they don't have anything in their life that needs to be fixed.

I beg to differ we all have something that could use a little altering.

If you run across someone that fits that description, just pray that the Lord would shine a spotlight on their situation so their eyes are opened to the truth.

Self -esteem Worksheet

In order to have a healthy relationship with others an individual must first come to grips with how they see themselves.

Which is why I felt it was important to create this worksheet.

 Listed below are some questions to answer, in order to receive the best results you must be completely honest.

Now let's get started….

How do you feel about yourself?

What makes you stand out from others?

Has there ever been a time you didn't believe in yourself?

Do you ask for help when you're feeling down and out?

Are you afraid to make mistakes?

Are you ashamed of anything you've done in your life?

Do you seek validation from others?

Are you afraid to step out of your comfort zone?

Do you gossip about others?

Have someone hurt you and left you with unforgiveness in your

heart?

Rebuilding character

To rebuild anything not to mention yourself takes time and patience.

Just imagine how much more it will require you to build torn relationships with others. In this exercise you will start with rebuilding yourself and ultimately use it to help build what was broken with others.

1. Stop comparing yourself to those on social media, or those you see around you every day.

2. Always find a way to compliment yourself rather it was for something big or small.

3. Eat right so that you feel good about the progress you're making in your mind as well as your body.

4. Place yourself around people that will support you in your need to be successful.

5. Your focal point should always be on the things that bring you enjoyment.

As we do those things above, we will be able to start repairing what caused our relationships with our sister's to become damaged.

When we spend time comparing ourselves to others we lose the drive in us to be productive.

How can we compliment anyone else when we can't compliment ourselves.

Not thinking how overeating causes us to find fault in everyone and everything else in attempt to take the attention off ourselves even if it's for just a moment.

In order to be successful, you have to surround yourself with likeminded individuals and lastly you know what you enjoy so why wait for someone to come up with something and it isn't what you want.

POETIC STATION:

PUSH PAST THE PAIN (POEM)

No-one said this life would be easy nor told you'd have to carry
this burden alone.

Your life has been a testament look how much you've grown.

Grown not in the ways you thought, but in ways you may never
know.

If a storm never comes your way, how do you expect to grow?

My ways aren't yours, neither your ways mine.

You've spent too much time trying to figure things out of your
control.

Then wonder why there's no rest for your weary soul.

Broken hearts do mend when you leave it be.

The answers to your problems are found on your knees.

There you would find many keys.

Keys that would unlock the treasures that held your future.

It's you that's kept yourself from succeeding by continuing to live
an illusion.

So, it's evident you push past this pain that hinders you from flying.

Your wings are meant to soar beyond what you see.

The Creator promised to give you an eternity if you'd believe.

Believe you are a fierce warrior that would cause the atmosphere around you to change.

Say the word and the yokes of bondage will fall off you.

Stop refusing to tap into your strength it only allows the enemy to prevent you from receiving your breakthrough.

-Push past the pain

FATHER (POEM)

Father,

I come humbly before the throne regarding my sister for she
needs a touch only you can give.

How can I prove to her she's valuable and it's time she accepts it
and live?

I want to be the sister she needs when the world she knows have
turned its back.

To be the one she goes to when her character is suddenly under
attack.

I may not have all the answers, but the only way not to get a
response.... is if you never ask.

So, it's okay to require about how you can be redeemed from your
past.

The creator says he has cast those trials into the sea and
remembers it no more.

The enemy may come buffet you but will never be able to break
you.

Ignore the lies he has spoken over you and embrace the fact that your sins have already been forgiven … have already been washed away.

Believe that you've been chosen and cleansed by the blood of the lamb.

A sacrifice that could only be given by the lord of all….

The Great …. The Great I am.

We all have fallen short of God's glory, but that's not the end of our story.

Our story is still being written each day we are blessed to open our eyes.

The father loves us enough to reach beyond our brokenness and rain down blessings from the skies.

The rain will wash us from the impurities we have received from the world.

All is asked is that we don't allow the swine to have access our pearls.

People that never meant us any good just sent to distract us from receiving our rightful inheritance.

There's evidence that shows our price is far above rubies.

We have been given beauty for ashes to demonstrate how far we have come.

Now let's reach back and grab our sisters for she still has a race to run.

Our job has always required us to cheer her on every step of the way.

So just in case she should stumble; instead of assassinating her character, we must take a knee and pray.

Pray that the father's plan for her life will soon be done.

Can you hear the angels rejoicing over her… for she was once deemed the lost one?

Heaven has received another soul for the kingdom.

satan has been defeated we have the victory.

-Father

MY SISTER'S CROWN (POEM)

Fixing my sister's crown is for all of us to do.

It hasn't been assigned to only to me, but also to you.

You must rise above the mentality of thinking you're better than the rest.

Because when God created women…He created the best.

Not to be sex symbols or even be trophies that can be easily placed on the shelf.

But to know yourself worth if nothing else.

For too long we have put each other down by word, thought, or deed.

We must start rebuilding by pouring into our sister's that's what we need.

How did we get to the place where we felt competing was the only way to succeed?

This way of thinking has caused more damage instead of us being set apart not to mention being set free.

Free to come together and take this world by storm.

We've got in the way of ourselves by doing it all wrong.

We have allowed society to shape us mentally and physically,

instead of by the potter and wonder why we break so easily.

We have made ourselves believe we could do things on our own.

By pushing order out of its place and question why we're alone?

There's nothing wrong with being independent and going after

what you believe.

It's when others and our minds trick us is when we become

deceived.

Why is it that the government can dictate how our homes are to

be?

They don't tell you that the missing piece is our men that had been

formed to be the head of our families.

Telling us in order to make it you mustn't trust anyone but me....

the government: for it's us that control the strings.

If you refuse to embrace our policies, you can be replaced we

make no apologies.

We aren't here to be liked, but to manipulate your mind by us

calling the shots.

Ladies now that we know their tactics it's time we step out and kick over this box.

If we stop with the foolishness, we'll understand we're stronger than the enemy.

The enemy continues to cause some to neglect their responsibilities and kids just to name a few.

We must put away being bitter and jealous and make these demons confused.

Instead of discussing our sister's problems with those we see we ought to take it to our maker as we fall on our knees.

Tell him all about how she needs to be restored and leave it there.

Why gossip about her crown being crooked when each of us could use a repair?

It wasn't long ago there was a little tarnish, a missing diamond, and a chip was noticed on yours.

So why are you so quick to call your sister out and bring attention to hers.

We all have had hardships/shortcomings in which we had to bear.

Rather we want to believe it or not in order to make it we must give it our best shot we all have been there.

Allow love to be our compass to guide us back to our rightful place.

Get rid of our ratchetness and replace it with grace.

Refuse to get by…. by holding our heads held high.

Instead of being torn down with separation we must start the process of restoration.

Choose to speak life oppose to detriment in the lives of others.

Our children are looking to us as leaders…. We all are mothers.

Mothers rather by blood, adoption, or those we encounter daily.

What would people say of you if your life ended suddenly?

Would they see you as someone that made a difference or someone that refused to help their sister because she was too caught up in her own appearance.

Appearance that can be here today and gone tomorrow.

Simply because you've become vain and shallow.

How did we get to the point of placing our integrity into a bottle?

A bottle that sealed our brokenness and sorrow all while being tossed into the sea.

My sister, our crown was never given to outshine the women next to us, but instead assist her to go after the things that would cause her to succeed.

Success that would produce nothing less than greatness.

Greatness beyond all she ever witnessed.

Assure her that all she kept under lock and key, you'll be a keeper of it all for an eternity.

For a sister will never be someone that would expose secrets, share her sister's nakedness: for the entire world to see.

Fixing your sisters crown is a job we must take seriously.

When will we stop allowing others to separate us, paint a distorted picture of how they view us, and come together and change by building each other up.

Brick by brick, one by one, there's so much work that needs to be done.

Fixing my sisters crown is for all of us to do.

It hasn't only been assigned to me, but also for you.

- My Sisters Crown

.

CHAPTER EIGHT:

SCRIPTURE KORNER

The scriptures are written to strengthen our spiritual man so that we can stand in the face of adversity and not be defeated by the hands of the evil one. So even in our weakness our God is strong. May these scriptures detailed in II Corinthians and Romans be of assistance in what you need to start your day.

II Corinthians 13:7-14 KJV

7)Now I pray to God that ye do no evil; not that we should appear approved, but that ye should do that which is honest, though we be as reprobates.

8)For we can do nothing against the truth, but for the truth.

9) For we are glad, when we are weak, and ye are strong: and this also we wish, even your perfection.

10) Therefore I write these things being absent, lest being present I should use sharpness, according to the power which the Lord hath given me to edification, and not to destruction.

11) Finally, brethren, farewell. Be perfect, be of good comfort, be of one mind, live in peace; and the God of love and peace shall be with you.

12) Greet one another with an holy kiss.

13) All the saints salute you.

14) The grace of the Lord Jesus Christ, and the love of God, and the communion of the Holy Ghost, be with you all. Amen.

Romans 14:

The passage reads:

10) But why dost thou judge thy brother? or why dost thou set at nought thy brother? for we shall stand before the judgment seat of Christ.

11) For it is written, As I live, saith the Lord, every knee shall bow to me, and every tongue shall confess to God.

12) So then every one of us shall give account of himself to God

13) Let us therefore judge one another any more: but judge this rather, that no man put a stumbling block or an occasion in fall in his brother's way.

16) Let not then your good be evil spoken of:

19) Let us therefore follow after the things which make for peace, and things wherewith one may edify another.

PRAYER

Master,

When I look into the mirror of my life, I don't recognize the person that I see.

I have betrayed my sister in a way that has caused her great pain.

So, I come to you today with a heavy heart, asking that you pour out your spirit upon me and cover my shortcomings in Jesus' name.

I don't deserve your grace, but I truly hope you'll forgive me for my part in tarnishing my sister's reputation and tarnishing her crown that has taking her years to attain.

My insecurities about myself have caused me to share things that were strictly for my ears only.

Off limits because if leaked into the wrong atmosphere things would cause an unwanted ripple effect.

However, this unruly member known as my tongue has now caused her secrets to become a part of the latest gossip.

Gossip according to oxford dictionary can be defined as casual or unconstrained conversation or reports about other people, typically involving details that are not confirmed as being true.

However, the information I shared were factual because it came directly from the horse's mouth.

It never dawned on me that I was gossiping due to the fact I didn't mention any names.

I didn't consider this type of behavior would cause so much turmoil in the life of the individual I called my sister and friend.

I'm not sure if this damage could ever restore the friendship, we had.

Time is said to heal all wounds, but what happens when that time never seems to come.

Tears that continue to fall with no-one there to help catch them before they hit the floor causing a mini flood to be found at your feet.

As a result, I step in it causing a bigger mess.

Father in heaven I ask from a sincere heart to be delivered from this pain and sinful act of selfishness and help restore my broken relationship with you as well as with my sister.

Sincerely,

_____

THANK YOU

I would like to thank you all for your continued support these past few decades.

It has been such a pleasure having you around to enjoy this beautiful journey with me.

I couldn't have imagined the Creator using me with just writing a few words to make a difference in the lives of others.

Since then, it continues to blow my mind that due to my obedience these words would come alive not only in me but on paper when I finally let go and allowed the holy spirit to guide me in what to speak. The bible states in I Corinthians 2: 9

But as it is written, Eye hath not seen, nor ear heard, neither have entered into the heart of man, the things which God hath prepared for them that love him.

Which is why I can't stop sharing what the Lord has put inside of me.

My purpose in all of this is to simply allow others the opportunity to experience the father in a way they never knew was possible.

Being open is the key for the creator would not force himself on you.

He stands as gentleman at the door of your life knocking.

You that must decide rather you will allow him access to come in.

If only one person receives what I have written, and it transforms their life in a positive way it'll be worth all the hard work endured in putting this project together.

We're instruments waiting patiently to be used, and who better to use us then the creator himself to accomplish what he has put in us to do.

I hope this mini guide blesses you as much as it has blessed me to write it.

Love always,

Your friend

Waldrena

Mrs. Waldrena Thomas-Robinson

ABOUT THE AUTHOR

My name is Waldrena Thomas-Robinson, a Florida native currently residing in the Carolinas with my amazing husband and three children.

I am a local published author specializing in inspirational poetry with a vast number of general writings in hopes of bringing love and restoration to those around the world.

For the past three decades I have orchestrated my craft of writing by realizing this gift was not intended to be hoarded but to share with the masses.

It's truly been a blessing to write about the Lord as well as give advice to people who needed guidance and reassurance.

It's never been about becoming rich or rubbing elbows with the elite but being able to share hope, and light on how awesome the Lord truly is.

I am not ashamed to admit that without the Lord's guidance I couldn't perform the way I have.

It's easy to pick up a pen/ pencil and scribble a few words on paper but being led allows the creativity inside of you to come alive and the birthing book process is made.

I count it a blessing that the unction of the Holy spirit guides my fingers as they gently stroke the keys that carefully penetrates the paper in such a way that leaves a trail of words behind causing not just myself to be in awe, but all who read them.

I have vowed to leave this world empty, for I know what I carry inside of me.

Which why I am bold in saying I can't and won't take to the grave the blessing bestowed upon me there's too many that need to be saved.

My assignment is greater than I could have ever imagined, I wouldn't trade it for anything in the world.

I look forward to continuing my writing journey if the Lord allows me to.

There's so much to share that will take all of us to do our part in order to reach the multitudes around the globe.

Again, I thank you all for assisting me on this journey of a lifetime.

Love Always,

Waldrena

Contact Me

Contact me for book inquires at:

awriterzkorner@outlook.com

Listed below are books/ prices available for purchase.

My sister's crown...$13.00

Finding Peace...A journey worth taking $12.50

Pen of a ready writer...$12.50

My pen is my weapon...$12.50

From the Abundance of the Heart..........................$11.95

Phony Bologna..$10.00

No more band-aids revealing the wounds................$7.00

Personalized Poetry...$5 & up

Shipping & Handling (via U.S. Media Mail) $4.00

Make all Checks payable to: Waldrena Thomas-Robinson All returned checks will occur a $25.00 fee. Cash app / Venmo are acceptable forms of payment.

Upcoming book: The glory behind my story

 Please include your full name, address, book title, and quantity of books you would like to purchase.

My greatest reward was being blessed with an amazing family.

Truly blessed beyond measure

My sister's crown

Made in the USA
Monee, IL
30 March 2023

30574868R00046